ILLUSTRATED BY

CARA MANES   FATINHA RAMOS

SONIA DELAUNAY
A LIFE OF COLOR

THE MUSEUM OF MODERN ART, NEW YORK

Charles was looking for his toy horse. He searched behind the chair, under the rug, and in every corner of his room.

He reached in the back of his dresser's top drawer and found, tucked in among his socks and trousers, a blanket made of fabric patches of many different colors. It looked familiar. It felt familiar. It even smelled familiar. But he could not remember why.

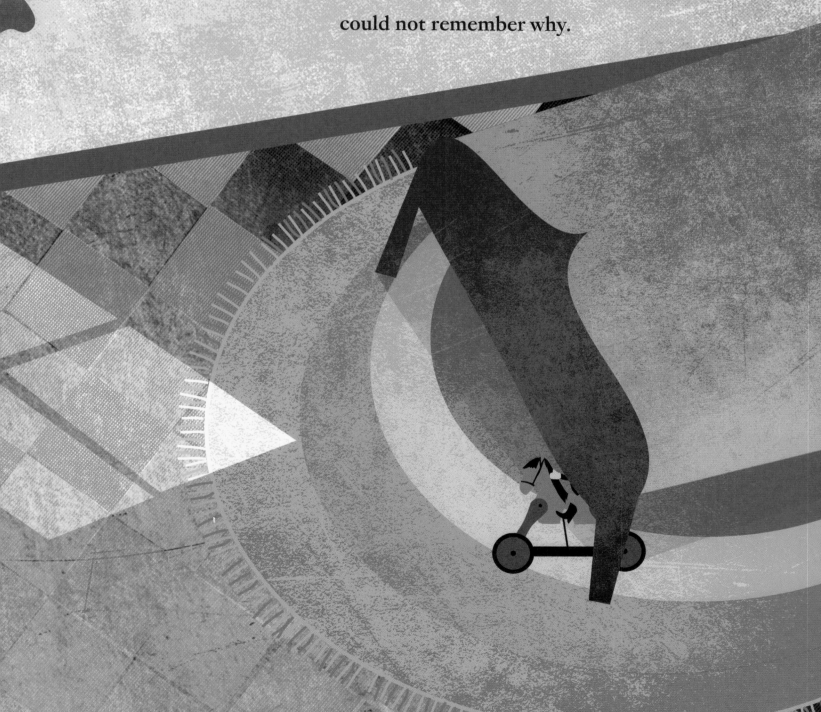

"Whose blanket is this?" Charles asked his
mother, Sonia. Sonia was an artist. So
was Charles's father, Robert, and many of
their friends.

"It's yours," Sonia replied. "I made it when you
were just born to keep you warm in your cradle.
It reminded me of the patchwork blankets
that people made in Ukraine, the place where
I was born, far from our home in Paris. But
your blanket is special. As I stitched together
the little pieces of fabric I could almost hear
the colors singing."

Charles pressed his ear to the blanket. "Mama, you must have really good ears because I can't hear anything!"

Sonia thought for a minute. "Your ears work just fine. But there are many different ways of listening."

"Your blanket changed the way I thought about colors," Sonia said. "When I listen to them, they tell me what to create."

"What do they tell you, Mama?"

Sonia thought again.

"Why don't we let the colors speak for themselves?" She took Charles by the hand. "Come with me!"

Their car roared as it zoomed through the streets of Paris.

Charles shrieked with delight as they barreled along, faster and faster. Suddenly the car lifted into the air. This would be no ordinary trip! Over the noise of the engine he yelled, "Where are we going?"

"Close your eyes," Sonia advised, "and follow the sounds of the colors."

When Charles opened his eyes, he was surrounded by bright lights and music and people dancing. He couldn't help himself: he tapped his feet and clapped his hands.

"This is Le Bal Bullier, where your father and I dance the tango. I always wear a colorful dress, and your father wears a grass-green jacket, a sky-blue waistcoat, and ruby-red socks."

"Papa sure can dance!"

"Try to feel the colors and the music together," Sonia encouraged. "When I painted Le Bal Bullier I tried to show everything, even things you might not think you can paint, such as the colors and sounds of movement."

"But I don't see Papa and you in the painting," said Charles.

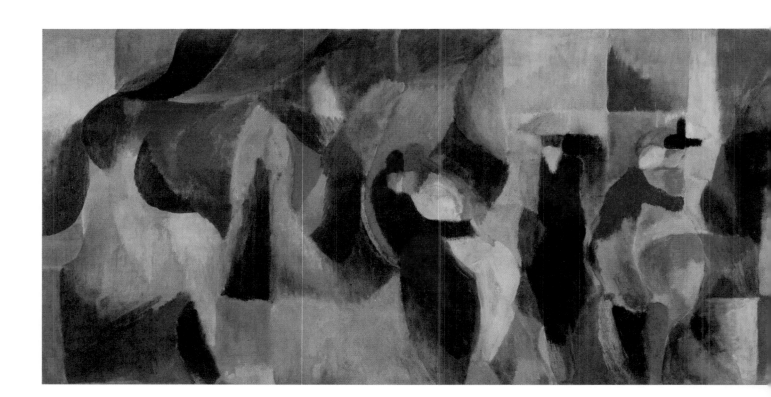

"You don't need to see me. And you don't need
to see Papa, or any of the other people, either.
In the painting the colors are dancing."

"But Mama . . ."

"Don't worry about understanding it now. Let's
go where the colors take us. Eyes closed!"

The sun was so bright that Charles could barely open his eyes. He felt his skin grow hot. He squinted and saw a busy marketplace full of fruits and vegetables, and he heard people speaking words he didn't understand. "Are we still in Paris, Mama?"

"Not anymore. I've whisked you away to Portugal, to a town where your father and I lived when you were a baby."

"We loved to visit this market. The foods here are different from those we have at home, and so is the way the sunlight looks and feels."

Sonia picked up a tomato. It was red and round. "Look at how the light changes the color of the tomato from one side to the other." Charles saw that one half was brightened by the sun, and the other, in shadow, was a deeper, darker shade.

"When I made this painting, I tried to capture all of the light, shapes, and colors of this busy place."

Charles looked hard. "The shapes fit together like a puzzle. One of them even looks like a hat."

"We have one last stop," Sonia said, as they
blasted off in their colorful car.

They zipped through the air. Charles felt the wind on his cheeks and watched the street lamps flicker in a city below. He saw bright colors in shop windows, he smelled bread from a bakery, and he heard the whoosh of trains and other cars.

All of his senses now swirled together. He was beginning to understand what his mother meant when she said she could hear colors, and feel them.

"We've just arrived in Amsterdam," Sonia said, "at a store that sells the fabrics I design."

"Do you see, Charles, how we experience all of these lights and colors and shapes and sounds that surround us at the same time, or simultaneously? I make designs for cars, furniture, and fabrics, because besides being looked at, art can be driven, sat on, or worn. Art is all around us, always."

"Can you imagine wearing a poem or an idea?" Sonia asked.

In a pile of clothes Charles spotted a pair of silk pajamas printed with one of Sonia's bright, bold designs.

"I want to wear an idea!" he said. "Can I try them on?"

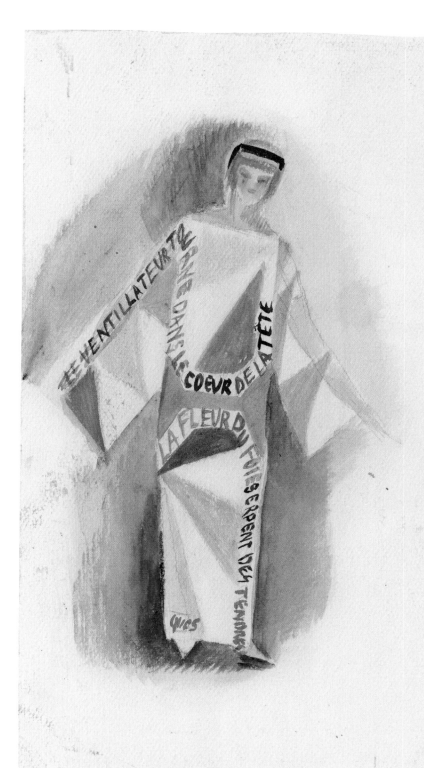

48

Charles pulled on the pajamas. The smooth, soft fabric slid over his skin. He felt weightless, as if he were floating. When he closed his eyes to think about all he had heard, seen, touched, and smelled, he imagined a rainbow of colors singing and dancing.

"It's getting late," warned Sonia. "And tomorrow is another day, with even more to discover."

"But Mama, I'm not sleepy yet! I have so many colors and sounds and ideas in my head!"

"I'm glad that the world has color to cover it
and keep it warm," Charles murmured dreamily,
"like a blanket."

"Now you know exactly what I mean,"
said Sonia, and she tucked him in and kissed
him goodnight.

Produced by the Department of Publications
The Museum of Modern Art, New York

This publication was made possible by the Nancy Lee
and Perry Bass Publication Endowment Fund.

Christopher Hudson, Publisher
Chul R. Kim, Associate Publisher
Marc Sapir, Production Director

Edited by Chul R. Kim and Emily Hall
Designed by Eva Bochem-Shur
Production by Hannah Kim
Printed and bound by Ofset Yapimevi, Istanbul

With thanks to Ingrid Chou, Isobel Cockerell, Cerise Fontaine,
Cari Frisch, James Heck, Elizabeth Margulies, Richard Riss,
Sarah Suzuki, Ann Temkin, Amanda Washburn, and Wendy Woon

This book is typeset in Central Avenue and Genath.
The paper is 150 gsm Amber Graphic.

Library of Congress Control Number: 2017937390
ISBN: 978-1-63345-024-0

Published by The Museum of Modern Art
11 West 53 Street
New York, New York 10019
www.moma.org

Distributed in the United States and Canada by Abrams
Books for Young Readers, an imprint of ABRAMS, New York

Distributed outside the United States and Canada by
Thames & Hudson Ltd., London

Printed in Turkey

Photograph Credits
Prismes électriques: Scala / Art Resource, NY
Bal Bullier: © CNAC/MNAM/Dist. RMN-Grand Palais /
Art Resource, NY
Portuguese Market and Robe Poeme No. 1329: Department
of Imaging Services, The Museum of Modern Art, New York
Portrait of Charles, Sonia, and Robert Delaunay:
Courtesy Pracusa

SONIA DELAUNAY

Sonia Delaunay-Terk was born Sarah Stern in 1885, in Gradizhsk, Ukraine, and was raised in St. Petersburg, Russia, by the family of her uncle, Henri Terk. After studying in Germany, she moved to Paris, France, in 1905, where she met and married the artist Robert Delaunay. Together, and in conversation with the artists, writers, and other thinkers who had gathered in that vibrant cultural center in the early 1910s, they proposed a bold idea for their art. Instead of depicting people, places, and things as they appeared in real life, the Delaunays were interested in reflecting the modern world by capturing its colors, shapes, sounds, and movements. To describe their experiments with color and form they used the term Simultanism (*simultanéisme*) to express the idea that the bright, bold, contrasting colors of their compositions had a particular effect on each other when experienced at the same time. The poet Guillaume Apollinaire, a friend of the couple, called their project Orphism, after the Greek mythological musician Orpheus, because of the relationship between the sensory experiences of sight and sound in their artwork. Music played an important role in the Delaunays' lives. In fact, their son, Charles, born in 1911, grew up to become an expert in jazz music.

Delaunay-Terk believed that art touches all parts of our everyday experiences, from the clothes we wear to the objects we use. In addition to paintings, she also designed and produced fabrics and other products until her death, in 1979, at age ninety-four.

Prismes électriques (Electric prisms). 1914
-
Oil on canvas, 8 ft. 2 7/16 in. × 8 ft. 2 7/16 in. (250 × 250 cm)
Musée national d'art moderne/ Centre de Création industrielle, Centre Pompidou, Paris

Portuguese Market. 1915
-
Oil and wax on canvas, 35 5/8 × 35 5/8 in. (90.5 × 90.5 cm)
The Museum of Modern Art, New York. Gift of Theodore R. Racoosin

Le Bal Bullier. 1913
-
Oil on canvas, 38 3/16 in. × 12 ft. 9 9/16 in. (97 × 390 cm)
Musée national d'art moderne/ Centre de Création industrielle, Centre Pompidou, Paris

Robe Poeme No. 1329. 1923
-
Watercolor, pencil, and gouache on paper, 14 1/2 × 9 3/8 in. (36.9 × 23.7 cm)
The Museum of Modern Art, New York. Purchase